MEET THE AUTHOR
– SHOO RAYNER

What are your favourite animals?
Cats – what else?

What is your favourite boy's name?
Max

What is your favourite girl's name?
I love all girls' names!

What is your favourite food?
Cheese

What is your favourite music?
Prince

What is your favourite hobby?
Plumbing and plastering

What is your favourite website?
http://www.shoo-rayner.com

For Lindsey and Colin

Contents

Chapter 1
Guys from the Sky

I bet you saw that TV programme about me and my island and I bet you had a good laugh. Everyone did. Well, I can tell you that the programme was all lies! I am writing this book to tell you what it's really like.

Craig M'Nure's my name and manure's my game. I make my living out of bird poo. I'm proud of what I do.

Let me tell you how it all began.

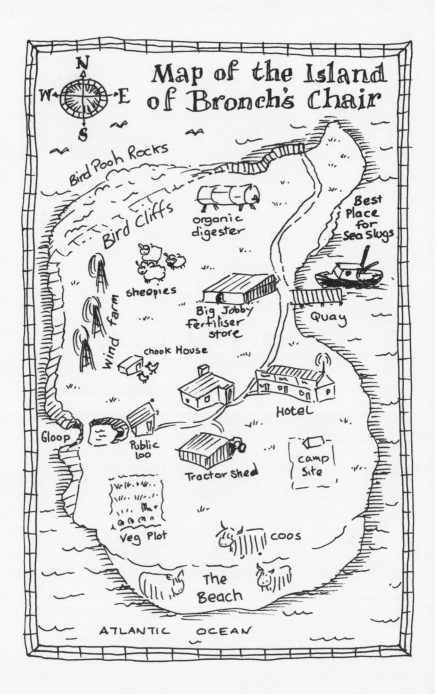

I live on a wee island in the middle of the Atlantic Ocean. I scrape bird poo off the rocks. I put the poo into bags and send it to my cousin in Scotland. He turns it into the best garden manure. We call it "Big Jobby".

My father made manure this way, and my grandfather, too. Once you've eaten a potato that's been grown in Big Jobby, you'll understand just how well I do my job. I feel proud that this is the way I spend my life.

Not a lot happens on my island. Sometimes we get visitors who come to study the amazing wildlife. They're mostly the outdoor sort. They bring tents and camp.

By the way, when I say we, I mean myself and my wee dog, Angus. You mustn't think that I'm a lonely old fool who talks to himself!

Now and then, something odd happens on the island. I know it's miles from anywhere, but you can never be sure what will turn up.

One day, from out of the sky, a helicopter turned up. It landed in my yard. This island is famous for its strong winds, but the blast from the blades of that helicopter almost blew the house down.

Some big guys got out. They wore bright orange suits and helmets. They looked like aliens or something. Angus went barking mad!

The guys were from the phone people. The island had been used as a half-way station for the phone cable to the USA. This cable was laid across the Atlantic Ocean in 1952. We've had free phone calls ever since.

They told me that they wanted to lay a new cable across the Atlantic, a more modern one. It was to be a new super-cable and it was coming right past our front door! The INTERNET was coming to *our* island.

The new signal couldn't get across the Atlantic in one go. They had to have a booster station on *our* island. It would take them a few months to do all the work. So they asked if they could put up a hut and live here for a bit.

Soon, an even bigger helicopter came. The hut was hanging underneath it in several parts. It was much, much bigger than a garden shed. When it was put together, it was huge!

When all the work had been done and the cable had been laid, the men went home. The hut was left behind with the booster station in one corner. They said I could use the rest of the hut if I looked after the booster station for them.

The booster station was just a box that stood in the corner of one room. All it did was to flash on and off. But (and here's the best bit) it was connected to a computer with a link to the internet. And I could use it for free!

I've never been afraid of I.T. and I love playing with computers. So, it didn't take me long to get to grips with the internet.

Everything you need is there. If you don't know how to do something, there's either a website to explain it to you or someone you can email. People on the internet are very helpful.

Chapter 2
Website Madness

The winters are very, very cold on the island. Sometimes the wind blows so hard you can't stand up. The winter nights are long and dark. I was snowed up in my house for most of January. Poor Angus wasn't able to get outside at all, even for a pee! So I had plenty of time to work on my Craig M'Nure website.

The day my website went live on the internet was a bit of a let-down. I thought something would happen right away, but nothing did. I had hoped the whole world would want to have a look at it. They didn't.

But the next day, I had my first email. It was from a Scotsman who lived in South America. He said my website made him feel like he was back home.

Then I had an email from a friend of his. Then I got emails from friends of his friends. Before long, I was getting more emails than I could reply to, from people all over the world.

There is one website that tells you who has the most visited website on the internet. Mine was soon among the most popular, and newspapers began to write about me.

Next I got an email from a TV station in London. They wanted to make a programme about me. They said there had been lots of programmes about people who had been left on islands. People liked to see how they coped.

They wanted to make a film about me! All I had to do was carry on doing what I did every day and they were going to film me. They seemed to be really interested in my work.

Now, I'm really proud of my work. I thought that this TV programme would be a chance to share my passion for poo with others. Also, it sounded like a bit of fun, and they were paying me well, too!

They asked where they could stay on the island. I thought about the phone people's hut – it had bunk beds and a shower. They could stay there.

I'd already had the idea of renting the hut to visitors. I told the TV guys they could stay at *my hotel*! They were going to pay me well for that, too.

When spring came, I began getting ready for the TV people. I painted the word HOTEL above the door of the bunk bed room. And I painted DINING ROOM over the door of the middle room of the hut, where the phone people had eaten their meals.

Over the door of the booster station room, I painted the words CYBER CAFÉ. I made a sofa out of old wooden boxes I'd found on the beach. I rigged up a windmill on the roof that gave enough power to boil a kettle. It took ages but I didn't want them to think I was stuck in the past!

The big day came. My wee dog Angus and I stood on the cliff-top staring out to sea. A tiny dot appeared. It was my cousin

Duggie bringing the TV crew to the island on his boat.

There were two of them. They were not good sailors! When they got to the jetty, their faces were the colour of puffin poo.

I thought that it was because they lived in London and never got any fresh air. But Duggie told me they had started off fit and healthy, but had been sick over the side of his boat ever since they set off.

Angus didn't like them at all. He stood at the water's edge and growled at them. I knew he'd bite their ankles if he could.

Duggie and I helped the two of them off the boat and laid them down on some sacks in my trailer. They groaned. They looked like two whales washed up on the beach!

****

I hitched the trailer to my tractor and drove up to the hotel. They wailed and grunted every time I went over a wee bit of a bump.

I showed them their rooms. I offered them some herb tea but they went green and hid under the bed covers. What odd people.

They must have been really ill. We didn't see them again until the next day. Duggie and I knocked on the hotel door to see if they were ready for breakfast.

"Good morning!" I said. "I've got some nice fried fish. I've got seaweed bread, or I could see if the hens have laid some eggs today. If you just want cornflakes I could go and milk a coo."

They turned that odd puffin poo colour again!

"Maybe a wee bit of porridge, then?"
I asked.

They ate some porridge. But they said it was too salty. They wanted sugar on their porridge – have you ever heard of such a thing?

While we ate, Duggie told them that the tide was coming up fast and it was time for him to go back. If they wanted to leave the island they would have to go with him now or wait for a whole week.

They smiled and said, "Thank you, but we've come to do a job and we'll finish what we've begun."

They stayed.

Chapter 3
The Gloop

They were called Alice and Simon. When at last they came out of the hotel the next morning, they were looking a lot better.

It was a lovely summer's day but they were wrapped up in bright red padded jackets as if it were winter.

"Is it always as cold as this?" Simon asked.

I looked around me. The sun was shining. A warm breeze was blowing from the south. "Cold?" I replied. "This is a heat wave!"

They said they had found the shower room but not the bathroom. I didn't understand at first and then I laughed.

"Oh, you mean the lavvy!" Then I had to explain about the toilets on the island. "All I've got is a hole in the ground, but I think you'd rather go to the public toilet. It's up at The Gloop. Follow the path and mind the coos."

"What's The Gloop, Craig?" Simon asked.

"Come on, Simon, I'm in a hurry," said Alice.

"Look out for the cow poo!" I yelled after them.

Too late. Simon trod in something and slipped. He swore.

When they came back, they had weird smiles on their faces.

Alice got her camera out and Simon told me how we were going to film the programme.

"What we want is to show your daily life here just as it is. We find it's best if you act as if we weren't here. Just do what you always do and we'll follow you around. If I ask you something, don't tell me, tell the camera. Talk to it as if it were your best friend."

A red light showed on Alice's camera and the filming began. "Action!" she called.

Simon smiled. "Craig," he asked, "can you tell us what a coo is? And what is The Gloop?"

Well, that was easy.

"A coo is an island cow," I said. "I've 20 of them. They live mostly on the beach. The food they like best is seaweed which makes their poo very rich and brilliant for garden manure.

"I put the coo pats into bags and dry them out. On cold days, I burn them on the fire and my wee house is soon nice and warm and toasty.

"And The Gloop," I went on, "is a tunnel that drops down from the top of the cliffs into a large cave.

"At high tide, the waves rush into this cave and shoot up into The Gloop.

"I built the public lavvy over the top of The Gloop, just where the tunnel comes out. It's quite a drop down into the cave, but it's all right if you've got a book to read and you don't look down.

"The tide washes the cave out twice a day so it's very clean. But you'll need to watch out and stand clear when the wind is blowing hard from the west. Then the waves shoot up out of The Gloop like a rocket!"

Chapter 4
Lights, Camera, Action!

Simon and Alice were not happy.

I wasn't happy either. They followed me around all day, like a pair of puppies.

They didn't know anything. They asked stupid questions all the time. And they were always finding things to complain about.

They complained that I didn't have any white bread. (I've always made my own wholemeal bread. It helps to keep my insides in order.)

They complained that there wasn't any soft toilet paper. (What's toilet paper?)

They couldn't sleep because up in the north the sun shines most of the night. And they hated the smell of bird poo. (What smell of bird poo? I can't smell anything!)

When they weren't making a fuss about something, they said nothing at all. They were filming all the time.

They would turn their backs to me and plan together. They said they were planning what to film next, but I knew they were plotting against me!

They were stuck on my island until Duggie came back.

So I just did my job every day and they followed me around and filmed me.

Chapter 5
The B52s

Millions of birds come back every year to lay their eggs on the island. Each pair comes back to the same old nest. For the last ten years, the same pair of gulls have nested on the roof of my house.

I call them the B52s after the American bomber! Every year, the B52s come back to nest just above my front door. Every day, Mr B52 waits for me to come out of the

house so that he can poo on my head.
Mrs B52 sits on the nest and cackles. Very
funny!

Well this year the B52s felt like a bit of a
change. They decided that Simon and Alice
were far more interesting targets to aim at.
The B52s moved their nest to the hotel roof
and I had a poo-free year.

Every time Simon and Alice poked their
heads out of the hotel, old Mr B52 was
waiting for them! Splat! He was a master
bomber and never missed. I think he was
aiming at their red padded jackets.

"Duck down!" I said.

Simon fell to his knees.

"No!" I told him. "Not duck down on the
ground! It's the *duck down* in your padded
jackets that annoys the birds. Mr B52 must

think you're a rival gull who wants to steal his nest!"

****

As I told you at the start, M'Nure's my name and manure's my game. I didn't know how much of my life was spent with poo until I had to talk about it to the camera every day.

During the long summer days, the birds fix up their nests and hatch and feed their young. There's a lot of poo to be scraped up.

There's a game I like to play while I collect up the coo poo. I call it tossing the coo poo. I choose a place to pile up the coo pats and mark it with a stick. Then I throw the coo pats at the target. When they're dry, they fly like frisbees. Angus likes to try and catch them as they fly through the air.

"Oh! That's so sweet!" yelled Alice. "Could you throw one at me so I can film Angus catching it?"

I chose a chunky one that Angus would find easy to grab hold of, and tossed it at Alice. "Angus," I called, "catch it, boy!"

Angus jumped for it but a gust of wind lifted it out of his jaws. It landed splat in Alice's face. It was crisp on the top but

soggy underneath. It didn't hurt, but Alice swore that I'd aimed it at her. I'm good, but not that good!

Oh, I've not told you about the Sheepies. You only find Sheepies on this island. They're not much use, but their poo does feed the grass on the island and that's what keeps it looking so nice and green. I told Alice and Simon not to stand behind them.

"Why?" Simon asked. "Do Sheepies kick?"

We were standing in the middle of a flock of them. "No, they don't kick," I said. "But when Sheepies poo, they shoot tiny, little pellets out with such force, they can hit a target 30 metres away."

Then, I saw one of their tails lift up. "Duck, Simon!" I yelled.

"Where?" Simon said.

The fool was looking in the sky for ducks.

It was too late. He was knocked to the ground by the force of the wee black pellets. His padded red jacket had black spots all over it where he had been hit. Those stains will never come out!

****

Simon and Alice met most of the bird life on the island.

The Pee Wee is a bird that got its name because it likes to wee on your head. Alice used up all her shampoo but the smell was still there.

Then there's a kind of gull that only lives on this island. It sicks up food for its young. It also spits a jet of vomit at anyone who comes too close. It's revolting stuff that can take the paint off a door. It took the shiny silver finish off Alice's camera!

Chapter 6
Curry Surprise!

Once or twice we nearly had a punch-up. It was clear that Simon and Alice blamed me for everything.

All week they complained about the food I cooked for them. The day before they left, I heard Simon telling Alice that he couldn't wait to get back to London so he could go out for a curry.

"Oh, you like curry, do you?" I asked. "I can cook curry! As it's your last night on the island, let's have a party to show we're good friends." I didn't want them to go home in a bad mood with me.

I spent the whole day working hard to make the curry. It was my very own recipe. There's nothing quite like it to clear out your insides.

"This is great!" Simon said. "You should open a place in London and sell this stuff. What's in it?"

I didn't tell him. Sea slugs are very tasty but they don't look very pretty until they're cooked. Then they look a bit like chicken.

"Oh, it's the very best seafood that the island has to offer!" I said, and smiled sweetly.

They seemed to be really grateful that I'd made such an effort and soon we were joking about all the ups and downs of their week-long stay.

The curry was great. Simon had two helpings!

I went home early and left them to get a good night's sleep before they set off for home the next day.

As I left the hotel, I looked up at the sky and saw dark clouds. I knew that bad weather was coming.

"There's a gale blowing up from the west," I called out to them, as I shut the door behind me.

It was a terrific storm. At first Angus slept through it. Then, in the middle of the storm, as the lightning flashed and the rain lashed against the windows, Angus started to growl.

I know all his growls, and this one was telling me that Simon was out and about.

I looked out and saw the light from Simon's torch sway to and fro, as he fought his way up to The Gloop.

This was not the night to need the lavvy. I put my waterproofs on and fought my way to The Gloop, too.

It was the worst storm on the island since 1972. I tried calling out to Simon, but the wind was too strong.

I fought my way to the lavvy but I was too late. Simon was already inside. The wind was howling all around me, but I could still hear him groaning. He must have eaten too much curry. (I told you it cleared out the inner tubes.)

I looked out to sea. The rain was battering my face. Then, suddenly, a huge wave loomed out of the dark. It was racing towards the cliffs and the cave down below. I banged on the lavvy door and yelled, "Simon, you've got to get out of there now!"

"Urrgh!" was his reply.

The wave crashed into the cliff, filling the cave with water. There was only one way for it to escape.

I heard the water rush up the tunnel of The Gloop. A great fountain of water blasted out of the roof of the lavvy. Riding on top of it, with his trousers round his ankles, was Simon.

I've never seen anyone look so shocked.

Chapter 7
Fame at Last

Simon and Alice didn't come over for breakfast the next day. They took all their things down to the jetty and waited for Duggie to come and get them. They didn't even say goodbye.

I could have told them there was going to be a very high tide expected that day. But I didn't bother – I was fed up with them, too. Angus and I watched as the water rose over the jetty and washed away their cases.

Luckily, the tide was coming in, so the cases were washed up on the shore among the seaweed. Simon got very wet rescuing them. He slipped and fell into a rockpool.

At last, Duggie's boat came to take them home. Simon and Alice were in a great hurry to get their things on board.

As the boat set off, I heard Simon say, "We're free! We're safe! We're going home at last!"

He had forgotten the B52s. With the sun behind them, the gulls swooped down on one last bombing run. They left Simon and Alice a present to take home with them.

Simon swore at them.

They took a lot of film back to London.

That's how they got their own back on me. We didn't have TV out here in the old days, but now there's the satellite I get to see everything.

They made a fool of me.

The programme showed me at my work talking about poo like it was my whole life.

But I've got lots of other interests – like wind power for example. That's where all my electricity comes from.

I had hoped that people would see the programme and would want to come and stay at my hotel.

When I saw the programme, Simon and Alice had made it look as if it was just an old hut. *No-one would want to come and stay on the island the way they showed it,* I thought.

Well, I got so angry, I sat right down and wrote this book to tell people what it's really like here. Then I felt a whole lot better.

A lot of people watched that TV programme and my website became the most popular in the world. I even got into the record books.

A lot of people wanted to come and visit the island and stay at the hotel after they saw the film and visited my website, www.shoo-rayner.com. The hotel is booked up for the next three years!

Such interesting people want to come to stay. There are bird watchers, manure experts and others who are looking for the simple life and good, fresh island cooking.

They all love my curry and they all go home with hats to remind them of the island. The hats have "I survived the B52s" printed on them.

So my island is famous now. It just goes to show that the old saying is true – "it's an ill wind that brings no-one any good!"

GIFTS FROM THE ISLAND

SURVIVED THE 65'S

Bronch's Chain CURRY
yum!

SUGAR SHEEPIE POOHS.

BIG JOBBY FERTILISER

ISLAND COO

B52

Who is Barrington Stoke?

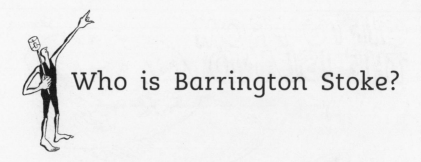

Barrington Stoke went from place to place with his lamp in his hand. Everywhere he went, he told stories to children. Some were happy, some were sad, some were funny and some were scary.

The children always wanted more. When it got dark, they had to go home to bed. They went to look for Barrington Stoke the next day, but he had gone.

The children never forgot the stories. They told them to each other and to their children and their grandchildren. You see, good stories are magic and they can live for ever.